THE CARNIVAL OF DOOM

SEQUEL TO THE LIBRARY OF SOULS

THE CARNIVAL OF DOOM

Copyright © 2018 by Richard Denney

[Juvenile fiction – Paranormal – Horror – Friendship – Family – Ghosts – Adventure
Mystery and detective stories]

ISBN: 978-1539186250

Printed and bound in the U.S.A.

CHAPTER 1:
DO YOU LIKE CLOWNS?

The town of Pottinger, Massachusetts is supposedly haunted by a murderous clown named Grimshaw. Uncle Monty thinks it's a load of crud, but that's because he's deathly afraid of clowns and he's trying to act like it doesn't bother him. He's see his fair share of demonic crazies, but he refuses to believe that an actual ghost of a clown exists... well, guess we're about to find out. I mean, after escaping with our lives from a demon-infested public library, we really shouldn't be surprised for anything.

Ever since we took care of Childermass Publi Library, which interestingly is only a few hours awa from this town, people know of us now. We've gotter more calls, our website has way more visits, and we even created an Instagram page, mainly for Monty's vain selfies because the man can't seem to get enoug of himself.

Speaking of Monty, he's standing right next to me, taking a picture of himself in front of Pottinger's public library with a giant smile on his face and a big thumb up.

"That doesn't make us look very professional," I tell him.

"It's for the gram, dude." Monty grins at me.

"Don't ever say those two things, ever again." I chuckle at him. He can be a character at times.

"I'm just trying to follow the trends. We've got over ten thousand followers on here, we have to keep up with the internet stuff. It's good for business." Monty smiles big and wide and hits the post on his picture. After straightening up his neon green tie, he trots up the steps of the library.

"Ok, Uncle Monty, whatever you say." I laugh and climb the first step of the library.

A chill riddles down my spine. It's only been a year since Childermass and going into a library makes me a bit nervous now. But I don't have a choice. The town's museum is located inside of the library and we were told by the town historian, Rose Zarr that the museum has a small section devoted to the lore of Grimshaw. Even though this town would prefer the stories didn't exist, it still seems to cash in on the legend. I guess you've got to make your money somehow, I mean, look at us.

Monty leads the way into the library and I'm hit with the strong scent of burnt coffee and books. The smell calms me down a bit as he heads toward the circulation desk. The inside of the library looks straight out of the 70s, everything is mustard yellow and pea green, even down to the linoleum-tiled ground. The desk seems to be made out of linoleum too, except it has that fake wood look and is all pocked up from moisture.

There are already three other people standing at the desk, a blonde girl who looks around my age but way taller than me, and a woman around Monty's age who has a bright purple pixie haircut. Next to her there's a stocky man with a long red beard and a duffle bag full of black and silver devices popping out from the top. One of the devices has blinking red,

een, orange and yellow lights and I instantly
cognize it.

It's an EMF meter, which is a device that ghost
nters typically use. We don't use them because I'm
sically a human EMF meter and they cause too
uch interference anyway.

I nudge Monty in the arm and he looks away
om his phone, over to the bag. I can see his neck
rn a bright red and I immediately regret alerting
m to my discovery.

Obviously, we're not the only "Ghost Talkers"
town and this doesn't seem like it will end well for
y of us.

CHAPTER 2
NOT ALONE

Monty is angry and I am irritated. Monty hate working with other paranormal investigators so that's why he's angry, he doesn't typically play well with others. I'm irritated because this reminds me o Childermass when the other mediums showed up an things got crazy. So far, I'm not feeling too great about being in this town, but we need the money right now. We can't keep eating burgers and shakes and sleeping in smelly motels for another year. I think we need an RV, Monty says he wouldn't be caught dead driving one.

"Rose didn't tell us there were going to be other people investigating this clown business. This is just like Octavia-" Monty stops himself from talking and looks down at me. "Sorry."
"No, it's okay. I can't keep being scared of what

appened." I smile at him, letting him know I'm okay hen I know I'm not, at least not fully. "And we'll st keep our distance from them, or at least try."

Well, here's hoping," Monty puts a fake smile on as he purple haired woman heads over to us. Damn it.

Hi," she says. "I'm Rachel Farrow and this is my iece, Danni, and our case handler/extra investigator oomis. We were told that there would be two more f us here. The woman said a young boy and an older llow would be arriving later on today."

Older fellow?" Monty grits his teeth and I give a tiny tomp to his foot so he doesn't make himself look like complete idiot in front of strangers. He gets the int and folds his arms over his chest instead.

I'm Monty Santiago and this is my nephew Simon. Ve work alone," Monty says. Just when I thought he vouldn't do something stupid.

Well, so do we," Rachel smirks at Monty and rushes against his shoulder as she heads for the ibrary's exit, the red-bearded man and the blonde irl, Danni, right behind her. Before they head out of he door, Danni turns to me and smiles.

Good luck," she says and hurries out the door before

I can tell her the same thing. At least she doesn't seem to hate us right now.

I turn to Monty and shake my head.

"What?" he acts like he doesn't know what I'm talking about.

"Really? *We work alone.* We're not in competition."

"No, but if we can get rid Krusty the Clown before they do, we might get a bigger check." A giant smile spreads across Monty's face as he turns back toward the circulation desk and begins his infamous smooth talking.

"Ay dios mio," I say under my breath and head over to the desk to join Monty.

A few minutes later, we're standing inside of the museum and boy is it small as heck. They charge $2 for the regular museum, but for the inclusion of the Grimshaw section it's an extra $3, I knew they made some money out of this. Before we head into the room, the woman from the desk pulls on some gold rope and a dark purple curtain peels away from a large display.

"Are we about to watch a magic show?" Monty whispers to me.

"I guess they like it to look mysterious, so people will want to see what's behind the curtain," I explain to Monty as he combs a free hand through his hair and puts on a smile for the woman.

"Thanks again," he smirks at her as she walks past us and closes the museum door behind her.

"You're gross," I shake my head at him and proceed further into the room.

There's a child-size statue of a deer and a few science fair-like displays of historic events set up. Everything looks cheap and as if it was put together by third graders. The displayed events range from Elvis Presley staying at the Penny motel, the one we're currently staying at, and a carnival that took place every year until children and teenagers started to go missing back in the 80s and 90s.

I try to find a happier event because missing people doesn't really seem like something you'd want to promote in a town museum, it's a bit of a downer if you ask me. But there's nothing else, almost everything in the museum is super mundane, boring, sad and depressing.

"This town is pretty messed up," Monty says as he spins a makeshift carousel from the carnival display made of pink Popsicle sticks.
"You've got that right. Let's see what that Grimshaw display is all about so we can get out of here and get to work. I want to get out of this town as quickly as possible." And I'm not kidding. Even though we've only been here for a day, this place is making me miserable.
"You've read my mind," Monty says staring at a piece of toilet paper signed by Elvis Presley.

It doesn't take us long before we're standing in front of the display devoted to Grimshaw the clown. The main feature is a faded black top hat with the top of the hat being nearly burnt to a crisp. It's sitting inside of a glass case that has a set of heavy duty locks on it. A tiny white card inside of the case reads; *authentic top hat worn by Grimshaw before his demise in the clown disaster of 1955.*

Funny enough there isn't much on the internet far as research goes for the Grimshaw case. I und an article about a missing teenage girl named atasha Ward who went missing during the last rnival in 1996 and a few vintage photographs volving clowns and Halloween.

Other than that, there wasn't much else about hat has happened in this town. Rose Zarr also was ry tight-lipped about everything. She said she'd plain more over breakfast tomorrow morning. I st hope this doesn't have anything to do with monic stuff, I'd prefer not to mess with any of that uff for a while, if I can help it.

Since I forgot my camera in the car, which rely happens, I borrow Monty's phone and take a w pictures of the display so that I can look stuff ver back at the motel.

This looks more put together than anything else in he museum," Monty says as he picks up a plastic lder that's full of photographs and articles about issing children and teenagers. The folder looks thick, which means no one on the internet cared enough to share this stuff, or the town is trying to keep most of what's happened here as local as possible. I start snapping pictures of the articles wit Monty's phone and feel a familiar tingle on the back of my neck.

Slowly, I turn and on the other side of the large window showing the parking lot, a young boy staring at me. I watch as he leans forward and huffs hot air onto the window, creating a slate of fog and begins writing something on it. After rubbing the last word into the glass with his finger, the boy vanishes into thin air. Taking a step back I nearly crash into another display as Monty grabs me before I cause real damage.

"Simon, what's wrong?" he shakes my shoulders. Without saying a word I point to the window and Monty sees what the boy has written:

He's gonna get you.

CHAPTER 3:
CLOWNING AROUND

Back at the motel, I've yanked the curtains shut and am sitting with the TV blaring in case any spirit feels like making a surprise appearance to me right now. I'm not in the mood for anything crazy and just when I thought this wasn't going to be that bad of a case, I was proved super wrong. I just hope doesn't get worse.

"So, how about pizza?" Monty is rummaging throug the motel's phonebook with his reading glasses on, something he hates for even me to notice. He refuses to get glasses or contacts, he thinks it will cramp his style, which I didn't even realize was a thing.

"Pizza sounds good, especially after that message at the museum."

"After what happened in Childermass, I think we ca

handle pretty much anything. But if you feel like we can't do this, just tell me and we're out and I'm serious."

I turn to uncle Monty and stare at him for a moment. He isn't looking at me, he's still reading the phonebook. Ever since the library of souls nearly stole ours, he's become a completely different person. I mean he's still arrogant and can be a pain in the butt sometimes, but we've grown super close and even though I sometimes wish we never went to that library, I'm grateful that it brought me and Monty together.

I guess we just didn't realize how much we needed each other and that feels good to know. "I'll let you know," I tell him, watching as he flips a few more pages. "You know you can use your phone, right?" I tease Monty. He finally looks up from the phone book and looks at me over his glasses. "No matter how cool I think the internet is, a good old phonebook is ten times easier for finding local pizza joints." Monty grins, pulls out his phone, and begins to dial a number.

The TV catches my attention with an announcement of a horror movie marathon starting in a couple of days, October 30th. We should've known that coming to a haunted site in October was a bad idea, also because this month seems to take a lot of energy out of me. It's like all the spirits know I'm extra vulnerable around Halloween-time and think I'm a free energy buffet, I freaking hate it.

In the morning we're meeting Rose Zarr at Pugg's Diner, a locally famous breakfast, and burger restaurant. This time around I'm not taking any chances, I want to know everything about Grimshaw and this town. After what happened in Childermass, Monty and I took five months off and stayed with his friend in Texas. The break was good for me, I was able to rejuvenate and chill out.

When Monty told me people were trying to hire us for new cases, I felt like I owed it to Monty for taking care of me for so long and told him I was ready. But I wasn't. We took on six cases before getting the call about Grimshaw and I made sure they were easy cases, a few simple haunted houses, a

ayground haunted by a school bully, and an old
oman who just wanted to watch over her daughter.
er daughter mistook her for an evil spirit.

Even though those cases were pretty easy for
e, I still wasn't 100% ready to handle just anything.
o when Monty told me we were coming to
ottinger, I almost told him that I wanted to quit it
l. But later that night I had a dream about my
arents. They told me that I was needed more than
aything and that my "gift" wasn't meant to be given
o on. When I woke up the next morning I just
niled at Monty and gave him the okay.

That's why I'm still in this town. If my own
arents think I can do this, that I can keep going and
elp people, then I will keep trying until I can't
aymore.

The pizza should be here in thirty minutes. I'm
oing to jump in the shower." Monty says as he
athers his towel and "special" shampoo, which helps
row back his hair, and saunters into the bathroom.
. minute later I hear fifties music playing from

inside the bathroom.

Monty's left his phone on the bed, the speaker in the bathroom connected via Bluetooth to his phone. I decide to go through the photos to see if I can gather more info before seeing Rose in the morning.

The first photo I open up is of the display. There's the top hat in the glass case, a paper Mache red balloon, and a jar full of foam clown noses. The next photo is of Grimshaw himself, except someone has purposefully etched out his eyes with a black marker. I didn't notice that before in the museum. He looks completely maniacal and demented.

Quickly, because the photo of Grimshaw is really creeping me out, I open up another photo. This one is the first page of the binder Monty was looking through before I flipped out about the dead kid at the window.

It's a timeline of events that led up to an "accidental fire" at the old doll factory, but in 1955, it was known as The Clown House, which housed all

ıe clowns and carnival performers back in the 50s
hen the carnival in town was at its most popular. It
oesn't say anything else about the fire or how it was
arted. Now I have more questions to ask Rose.

I swipe through the next few photos with little
) no important information about Grimshaw. It's
ıostly all about the missing children and how it all
:arted in the late 1940s when the carnival first came
) town. The next photo sends a shiver down the
ack of my neck. It's a photo of the foggy message
·om the dead kid at the library. Monty must've
ıken it before it could disappear. He's gonna get
ou... evidently, the kid means Grimshaw, but why be
ɔ vague about it? I hate spirits sometimes.

Obviously, Grimshaw is someone to be feared,
ɪccording to that cryptic message, but I'll make my
wn decision on this when I finally meet the clown
imself.

A rattle of knocks pummels the motel room
loor, startling me and making me drop Monty's
ɔhone on the floor, accidentally selecting a song

called Shake, Rattle, and Roll. The song plays at a higher volume from inside the bathroom but Monty doesn't seem to care.

I snatch the twenty dollar bill off of Monty's bed and head to the door. Grabbing the knob, something tells me to stop. *Don't turn it*, a girl's voice says in my head. This girl's voice is new; I've never heard her before. I let go of the knob and take a few steps back from the door.

An eerie chuckling begins from the other side of the motel room door, followed by a few more bangs. The doorknob rattles with so much intensity, I'm waiting for it to fall off of the door. The music in the bathroom grows louder and the bangs seem to be trying to keep up with the volume of the music.

"Go away!" I yell at the door.
This time high pitched laughter sounds from the other side of the door and I jump back, falling onto Monty's bed. Looking down at the bottom of the door, I see something red and shiny slipping through the crack. When it's halfway through I realize it's a

balloon. My blood instantly runs cold as the balloon hovers through the air, inflating all by itself.

"I said, go away!" I yell again, closing my eyes tightly, trying to focus on my ability. I can hear Monty trying to get out of the bathroom, calling out to me and banging on the door. Something is keeping him inside the bathroom.

Almost instantly the room goes quiet. The music is off and the only sound I hear is the rain that's started outside of the motel.

Slowly, I open my eyes and see a red balloon, floating directly in front of my face. It begins to spin at a rapid pace and then finally stops.

POP!

The balloon explodes sending a vat of ice-cold black goo right into my face. By the temperature and smell, I can tell it's ectoplasm. Just in time, the bathroom door flies open and Monty stumbles out, a worried look on his face.

"What the hell just happened?"

I scrape some of the goo away from my mouth and eyes with a towel and stare hard at the door, my teeth grit and my neck as hot as the Texas summer.

"*Grimshaw.*"

CHAPTER 4:
PANCAKES AND DEAD PEOPLE

The last time a spirit visited me in a motel wa
in Childermass. I feel like Grimshaw knows more
about me than I'd like and is trying to scare me awa
But after that balloon and ectoplasm mess last night
I'm more determined to get rid of this stupid clown
more than ever. I'm also trying to think about where
that girl's voice came from. She sounded older,
maybe in her late teens and she didn't feel
threatening.

Maybe she's one of the good ones. But then I
remember Childermass and my giant wall of trust
goes right back up. Not everybody is who they seem.

We're waiting inside of the diner for Rose. I'n
picking at a stack of chocolate chip pancakes and
watching the rain pummel down outside. It's getting

etty bad out there, I've stepped in so many puddles
nd Monty slipped and busted his butt when we
alked into the diner earlier. I just hope it isn't this
ad when we head to the carnival lot after breakfast.
Ve have to get to work as quickly as possible.

I had to take three showers to get that black
ctoplasm out of my hair and I still smell a little like
urnt paper. The only types of spirits that can create
lack ectoplasm are strong ones, which from the info
ve learned recently shouldn't surprise me. This
umb clown has scared this town so much that it has
bsorbed all that fear into energy and uses it to its
wn sick advantage.

For a moment I thought maybe we had another
ld woman just wanting some attention type case on
ur hands, but obviously, I was dead wrong.

Not only is this clown spirit evil, it likes to play
okes, and I hate jokes. Just ask uncle Monty. Earlier
his year for my birthday he got me a cake that
xplodes confetti. He didn't hear the end of it from
ne for at least a week.

The bell above the diner door pulls me out of my thoughts and I see a tall woman in a dark brown suit-dress heading our way. She's got on a pair of thick-rimmed glasses and her hair is blonde and in a ponytail. Of course, Monty straightens himself up before she gets to our booth.

"Monty and Simon?" she asks, her voice tiny and almost inaudible.

"Yes, ma'am!" Monty says gesturing for her to sit down.

Before she takes a seat she pulls a thick brown folder out from her shoulder bag and sits it on the table. A cloud of dust escapes from it, along with a photograph of a girl sitting on a carnival ride. A post-it note stuck to the bottom says it's Natasha Ward, the girl who disappeared in 1996.

"I'm Rose Zarr. We've spoken over the phone. The mayor wanted me to explain everything to you. He'd like the matter taken care of as quickly as possible. I've already spoken to The Farrow Agency. They were already at the old carnival lot this morning."

She begins pulling papers out of the folder and Monty's flirty look vanishes.

"If I may ask, why the need for two sets of paranormal investigators?" Monty snags a chunk of bacon between his teeth and chomps on it.

"As I said, the mayor wants this taken care of quickly. He'd actually like it to be handled before Halloween, which is why he asked for you. The Farrow Agency wasn't called on, they were actually already in town recording audio for their podcast. When the mayor learned about them, he inquired about their involvement. I suppose he figures with two paranormal agencies here things would move way faster." She looks at Monty, noticing that he doesn't seem too excited about working with other agencies. "Don't worry Mr. Santiago. You're both getting paid the same amount."

At the mention of money, Monty perks up and then goes back to acting like a gentleman. He's such a fart head sometimes.

"Thank you, Rose."

"Call me Ms. Zarr." She corrects him, her voice louder now. Monty goes as red as a strawberry. He hates being called out, but I love it. Feeling a little bit

29

better I take a giant bite out of the pancakes.

"Ms. Zarr," Monty says, looking embarrassed.

"Well, let's get started shall we?" Rose pulls a stack of yellowed papers out from the folder and clears her throat.

"In the late 40s, the town of Pottinger decided it wanted to open a year-round carnival. In 1947 the Pottinger Carnival hired a band of unemployed clowns from a closed down circus and several other sideshow performers. Three months later the carnival had its grand opening. About a couple of weeks after the carnival opened, three children went missing. A full year later a total of seventeen children had been reported missing in the town of Pottinger."

Ms. Zarr had to clear her throat again and rub the back of her neck before continuing on with the rest of the story. That's a lot of kids, more than I had thought.

"Nobody really had any idea that the missing children and the carnival were connected until an eleven-year-old boy came forward in 1955 and said that a mysterious man was performing an odd ritual in the woods behind the carnival lot. After investigating, the local police force found the man

rforming some type of demonic ceremony over a
rge pit. After apprehending the man, the decayed
odies of the missing children were discovered in the
t." Ms. Zarr pulls another stack of stapled paper
it of the folder and flips to the first page.
The man escaped the police car and several of the
olice officers, including a group of townspeople,
lased the man to the Clown House. There they
scovered the man was none other than Grimshaw,
le most popular clown at the carnival. It doesn't
ally say here how the fire got started but they made
lre that no one else was in the building but
rimshaw. He burned to death inside of the
lilding."

Monty exhales loudly and leans on the table.
Now, now that's some heavy sh-"
Monty!" I elbow him in the side.
t's heavy," Monty rubs his side and glares at me.
t is," Ms. Zarr says and puts the papers back in the
older. "After all of this happened and a girl was
ound alive in a shed attached to the Clown house,
hey closed the carnival and tried to put all of the
orrors of what happened behind them. But that

didn't work for long. Soon local children and even some adults were reporting sights of a clown near the carnival lot. But no officers apprehended anyone. Years went by with a reported sighting here and there but it wasn't until 1984 that things..." Ms. Zarr straightens herself up in her seat and stares down at her nails. She looks extremely uncomfortable talking about all of this and I don't blame her. Imagine living in a town this crazy?

She runs her tongue over her teeth and pushes her glasses back up the bridge of her nose.
"As I was saying, in 1984 seven children were reported missing, later being found in the Clown house, dead. By 1986 a total of twelve children and five teenagers were found dead inside that building. According to these records, it stopped again in 1986 and didn't pick back up until 1995. In 1995 no children were harmed, but three teenagers were found dead in the Clown House. Finally in 1996 one girl, sixteen-year-old Natasha Ward was reported missing and was later found..." Ms. Zarr rubs her forehead. I can tell she doesn't really want to talk about any of this anymore. But we need to know as

uch as we can. It's our job.

n the Clown House?" I ask. She looks up and nods.
Why didn't you explain all of this over the phone?"
Ionty inquires, folding his arms over his chest. He
oesn't look very happy.

Is. Zarr takes her glasses off and rubs at her nose.
The mayor asked me not to. He wanted to keep this
nformation confidential in a way. I know it sounds
ad-"

-Of course it does," Monty interrupts her. "This
ounds too insane to be true..." Monty takes a
noment and calms himself down. I rarely see him like
his, so it's making me a bit nervous. "I'm not sure we
an do this."

It's as if a giant bowling ball drops into my
tomach. *What did Monty just say?* He'd never pass
p a check, especially one this big.

We're willing to pay you extra." Ms. Zarr explains
s she pulls a piece of stark white paper out of the
older. It looks like she was already prepared for a
ayment increase.

It takes me a minute to realize what Monty is doing. He's about to give up this case, for me. Even though I really don't want to be here, I can't let him go through with this. I need to do this.

I need to get better, and to me, the only way I can is to face this insanity head on. I can't let what happened in Childermass ruin me. I won't.

"Monty," I nudge him in the shoulder. He turns to me, concerned and visibly upset. "We can do this."
"Are you sure?" he asks, looking at me directly in th eyes.

I hope to god I know what the heck I'm doing. "Yes."

"Good," Ms. Zarr says and places the piece of paper in front of Monty. "This is a simple contract stating that if anything happens to you... or your nephew in the process of this investigation, the town of Pottinger is not responsible." She's trying to smile but I can tell she doesn't agree with what she's even doing. It's clear this is all the mayor's doing.

Monty looks at me one last time and I nod, reassuring him that we'll work this out. For once in a really long time, I actually mean it.

I watch Monty signs the contract as an echo of Grimshaw's laughter erupts inside of my head.

CHAPTER 5:
HERE WE GO AGAIN

Pulling into the abandoned carnival lot, a sense
dread falls over me like an icy blanket. Monty
oks as if he feels the same. After the meeting with
s. Zarr at the diner, I feel like we've been ambushed
ith so much disturbing information that I'm still in
e process of taking it all in.

We've signed a few contracts like the one Ms.
arr presented to us but something about this
ntract felt unnatural, as if signing our names on it
eant giving in to the insanity that would soon befall
.

Purposefully Monty parks in front of the dark
een van next to an old ticket booth, blocking the
ar from easily leaving the parking lot. Even though
e knows we're being paid the same as The Farrow
gency, he's still not 100% happy with having to

work alongside them.

We'd prefer if you worked together on this, Ms. Zarr said to us before we left the diner. Monty cringed at her request and so did I. I wanted to keep as far away from them as possible and now, we'd be helping each other out. I just hoped they also knew what they were getting themselves into.

"I don't like having to work with them," Monty pouts, shutting off the car and crossing his arms like a grumpy toddler.
"I don't like it either, but we don't really have a choice," I explain to him as we get out of the car. I make sure to grab my camera, tossing the strap over my head and checking that the battery is full.

The lot is pretty bare except for the old ticket booth that looks like it's about to collapse at any moment and a huge carousel that has seen better days. It's rusty and almost all the colors of the horses and decorations have been washed out, possibly by the weather.

Interestingly there are still streamers twisted round the carousel poles. They flutter in the wind like dancing ghosts and an eerie feeling creeps up my back. The streamers must be from 1996, almost twenty years old. I can't believe they've lasted this long.

Something about this place feels off like there's something more going on than just a simple haunting. I mean a serial killer clown's ghost seems to be kidnapping people and killing them for some reason.

It doesn't make much sense and I'm eager to find out why exactly the spirit needs to kill people, usually scaring will give the ghost or demon enough energy to manifest and continue its haunting. They only kill if it benefits them because it takes so much energy out of them to do it. Something else is up, I just know it.

A hard tap on the driver's side window startles Monty and I. But it's just Rachel Farrow, with a huge grin on her face. Clearly ruffled by the scare he's just experienced Monty turns off the engine and exits the car, popping out a large black umbrella, even though it's stopped raining for a bit.

"Hey guys," Rachel says. "We've been here since nine and haven't discovered much. We're trying to find the Clown House but I can't seem to get a hold of Rose. Do you happen to know where exactly its located?"

"Nope, we didn't get that info from her either." Monty puts on a fake smile and shakes his head.

Rachel tilts her head and studies Monty for a moment.

"I'm sensing a bit of hostility from you," Rachel says. "We're getting the same check, Mr. Santiago. We're not here to shake up your gig, we're here because we want to help this town too."

Monty seems to be at a loss for words. Normally he's not used to being confronted about his personality or attitude and I want to give Rachel a round of applause for being able to pull it off. Finally Monty lets his guard down a bit and reaches his hand out to shake hers.

"Just call me Monty. Mr. Santiago makes me sound like an old man." Monty even conjures a real smile and I silently commend him for that.

"Call me Rachel," Rachel shakes Monty's hand and I sense something between them. There's something about Rachel that reminds me of my mom.

"So what did Ms. Zarr tell you about all of this insanity?" Monty strikes up a conversation with Rachel and I feel like this is my cue to explore the lot on my own.

I walk away from them and start taking a few photos of the ticket booth and a good one of the carousel. As I head over to the carousel, Rachel's niece Danni comes out from behind it. I make loud noises with my shoes letting her know that I'm coming her way so I don't startle her. She turns and sees me.

"Hi," I say, heading toward her. "I'm Simon."

"Danni," she says and shakes my hand. We zap each other with our energy and laugh while shaking our hands. Usually, it takes time to tell if someone is

41

a Ghost Talker, but on occasion, all the static energy from our abilities will cross and things like this happen.

"How long have you known about your gift?" I ask her. She has the bluest eyes I've ever seen and seems alive, unlike other people I've come into contact with

"Since I was seven-years-old. I almost died actually. Some old creep was haunting my grandma's house and was trying to hurt her, so I tried getting rid of him on my own and it got crazy. He tried possessing me and that was so not cool."

I laugh, not realizing if her story is meant to be a bit funny. I almost feel embarrassed until she chuckles. I like this girl already, well not like-like her. I don't like girls like that, but she seems really cool.

"Are you scared?" She asks me. I haven't been asked that in a really long time.

"A little, I think I'm just more worried about what's going to happen in the next couple of days. Something doesn't seem right."

"YES!" Danni startles me. "I think that too. There

ems to be more at play than just a scary clown
host. I just can't put my finger on it."

"I'm glad I'm not the only one who thinks that
then. After what happened to me and my uncle at the
Childermass Public Library, I have to be a little more
careful about things." The smile on her face falls.

"I heard about that. Your uncle was on a podcast
and talked about it. I'm sorry things got that crazy.
I've never been through anything like that except
when my parents died." Danni looks over toward her
aunt, who is still talking to Monty by his car.

"If you don't mind me asking, what happened?"

"They were on a haunting case in England and the
church they were trying to get the spirits out of
collapsed on them and their crew. You see, they
didn't have my ability, they just liked ghost hunting.
I had stayed behind with Rachel in Canada when it
happened. If they had taken me, maybe they'd still be
here."

"I'm sorry about your parents. I lost mine too when
I was little. It was a train accident caused by... a
demon." I felt my heart pummel into my chest. I
hadn't said that out loud since I first heard it at the
library.

"That's intense... I'm sorry." The look on her face makes me want to crawl underneath Monty's car and stay there. But I feel just as bad for her. It's just not fair. We should have our parents. Everyone should.

Trying to think of something to change the subject, I notice a rusty mirror on the carousel and in its reflection is a red balloon.

Without taking my eyes off of the mirror, I nudge Danni.

"Do you see that?" I ask, as she turns and looks into the same mirror.

"It's a balloon..." We look at each other and both turn in around in unison. The balloon is still there hovering in the air but it's not letting the wind take it. It's almost as if it's being controlled by something

"Where the hell did that come from?" Rachel and Monty head toward us. They can see it too, which means it's real. What the hell is going on here?

Before any of us can say anything more, the balloon begins to move away from us and toward the woods behind the lot.

"Rachel, I think I found- whoa, where did that

lloon come from?" Rachel and Danni's case
andler, Loomis comes out from a clearing in the
oods. The balloon stops at the broken metal gate
parating the lot and the woods.

"I think it wants us to follow it," I say.

The balloon moves forward, gliding past the
ate and into the clearing, where Loomis came out
·om. Without needing to say a word, all five of us
·llow the balloon, hoping to god that it's not leading
s to our demise.

CHAPTER 6:
THE CLOWN HOUSE

Usually, a mysterious red balloon leading five people into the woods would normally be a red flag to get the heck out of town, but not to people like us. We expect these types of things to happen and from the looks on Rachel, Danni, and Loomis's faces, they must deal with the same stuff while on their cases.

"Where do you think it's leading us to?" I ask Danni

"I have no idea," she replies, shaking her head. "But something about it feels icky and evil."

I think she might be right. Grimshaw is obviously playing with us and I just hope this stupid balloon isn't leading us to a bigger joke.

'We've been walking for at least a half hour, where is this thing leading us to? Monty groans, kicking at few pine cones on the ground.

As if answering his question, the balloon stops and just beyond a row of bushes, a giant red-bricked building looms down at us.

The balloon, seemingly content with its job begins to leave us, but before it can disappear into the woods, I turn my camera on and snap a quick shot of it as it hovers higher and higher above the trees.

"Nice camera," Danni says.
"Thanks," I smile. "I have a thing for pictures, especially taking them on cases. It's great for my collection and for our website."
"Awesome," Danni says. I'm just about to show her some of the photos on my camera when Monty takes the lead and steps through the bushes toward the building.
"So this must be The Clown House," Monty says.
"I mean, a red balloon did just lead us here, Monty."
Rachel laughs as she stops next to him and they look up at the charred windows and burnt shutters. You can clearly tell it had been on fire once upon a time. There's even a statue of a clown built onto the side of

e building. Everything about this place is creepy.

e all head closer to the building and I'm not sure if
s just in my head, but I swear I can smell burnt
ood. All the windows are blacked out but some still
ve glass. The front door is red, worn, and seems to
ve off a vicious energy as if touching it would send
1 electric shock through your entire body. I don't
ke this place, not at all.

This is incredible," Loomis says. "I've been
arching these woods to find this damn building for
burs and it's been right here all along." Loomis
oks like a mean biker dude, but right now he looks
ke a kid in a theme park. He starts taking pictures
mself. Now that I'm getting a better look at him, he
oks awfully familiar, like I've either seen him on TV
online before. I just wish I could remember.
Do we go in?" Monty asks.
suppose so," Rachel says. "Danni, what do you
nink?"

Danni turns to me and without her even having
) ask me, we both head over to the front door and

lay our hands, palms first, on the old wood. A rush of
an icy sensation flows through my veins and when I
turn to Danni, I see she's feeling the same thing.

"This place has a lot of energy, almost too much," I
say. "But I think with the two of us, we should be
able to handle it."

"I think so, too." Danni smiles and turns to her aunt.
"Just keep close to each other." Danni grabs the
doorknob and pushes the door inward. Since most of
the windows are blown out, there seems to be a lot of
light inside of the building, or at least on the first
floor.

After all five of us are inside, we start to look
around, Monty nearly clinging to Rachel and Loomis
recording everything on a red and black device. The
inside of the building is pretty disappointing for a
place called The Clown House.

The first floor is just an open space of concrete
with the skeletons of old metal twin beds, burnt to a
crisp, but still lined up.

"Is it just me or does this remind anyone else of a
concentration camp?" Danni says.

That's exactly what I was thinking," Rachel says touching one of the beds and some of the sheets still left behind.

I can see that now," I tell Danni. It's actually really unsettling.

I turn around looking for Monty and see him standing at the bottom of a rickety old metal staircase.

I guess this must lead to the second level."

And what about this?" Loomis says and we all look at what she's just discovered. It's a large square door on the ground behind the staircase.

It probably leads to a basement," Rachel walks over and starts pulling on the handle. After a moment of struggling, the door opens, shrieking like a horror movie victim. A flock of pigeons bursts out from the top rafts of the ceiling and Danni and I nearly scream our heads off.

It's just birds, kids." Monty laughs. But he looks just as unnerved as we just were.

Yup, just as I thought, a basement." Rachel declares and turns to Loomis. "Hand me a flashlight, please."

Quickly Loomis unclips a flashlight from his belt and

hands it to Rachel. Without a word, Rachel descend
down the hole in the ground.

"What the hell is she doing? It could be dangerous
down there." Monty runs over to the hole and leans
over it.

"I'm fine!" Rachel's voice echoes. "But this is totally
not a basement. It's a tunnel of some sort and it look
like it goes pretty far."

"Well, let's head down and see what the fuss is
about." Loomis takes a few flashlights out form his
bag and hands them out to us. He heads down first,
and then Danni and then uncle Monty.

I'm not usually one for venturing down creepy
holes in the ground, but if it helps us find out more
about Grimshaw then I think I'll be okay.

A stone staircase leads down into the tunnel. I
grab onto a bar that's been built into the wall and
take the steps down one by one. I'm not about to
break anything today.

When I take the second to the last step down, I
hear something crunch underneath my shoe and look

down with the flashlight. It's a mask, a clown mask. Creeped out but curious at the same time, I take my last step down from the staircase and snap a quick photo with my camera of the mask on the stairs.

I look down at my photo and notice that the mask is obviously vintage and is probably from the 50s. It might've even belonged to one of Grimshaw's victims.

"Yeah, nope," Monty says from behind me. "I didn't sign up for this. This reminds me of that horror movie My Bloody Valentine."

"Funny, I actually think this is an old mine shaft," Loomis explains. "But I didn't read up on any mine in Pottinger."

"Us neither," Monty's voice cracks. I've actually never seen him this scared and it makes me want to laugh, but I can't bring myself to embarrass Monty more than he's doing to himself now.

We watch as the beam of light down the tunnel heads closer and with our flashlights we shine them on Rachel as she heads toward us. Just then I see someone behind her. But they keep going in and out like a flickering candle.

Before I can say a word, Danni turns to me. "Who the heck is that?"

"I don't know," I tell Danni.

The spirit looks like a teenage girl and she's pointing at me.

Get out of here, if he comes back and finds you, you're all dead... the same voice erupts in my head. It's the same girl from the motel.

"Can you hear her, too?" Danni asks me. We can both tell the girl means no harm.

"Yeah, we need to get out of here."

"Rachel," Danni calls out. "I think we should go now."

On our way back to the lot, it starts to sprinkle. From that photo of Natasha Ward Rose Zarr had in her files, I'm 99% sure that spirit is her and just as I thought, she's one of the good ones or at least I believe she is. But we can't just leave.

e have a job to do and we'll be right back here in a
y or two ready to take Grimshaw down for good.
his clown has got to go. And if he's as powerful as
e think, we're going to need a lot more help and I
st so happen to know who to call about that.

CHAPTER 7:
A LITTLE HELP

The next morning at the motel Monty and I have one of our good friends Emerson Lewis on the phone. Emerson hates being on speaker but it's the only way he can talk to us both. When we got back to the motel last night after dinner at the diner, I knew we had to call Emerson. Even though we've been doing this for a long time, Emerson's been around longer and knows more about this stuff than we ever will.

"So what I'm thinking is that it's working with demon. No regular spirit can muster that much energy to murder so many people." The *It* Emerson is referring to is Grimshaw. I knew something else had to be up, there's no way Grimshaw could do all of this on his own. But it doesn't make me feel better. We've been trying to steer clear of demonic cases for

a while and now we've landed ourselves smack dab i
the middle of one.

"Do you think it's a good idea for us to stick around
Monty asks, pulling at his fingers. He's just as
nervous as me.

"You signed a contract dummy, you have no choice."
Emerson chuckles.

"But Simon is stronger than you think. Besides, this
sounds like a case I worked on back in '83. There wa
a school being tormented by the evil spirit of a
lifeguard that was drowning kids in a school's pool.
The lifeguard was had a demon's help and it took us
three weeks to realize what we needed to do..."

Emerson stops talking and there's a long silence.

"Well, what did you need to do? Now's not the time
for your dramatic pauses, Grandpa Munster." Monty
snaps but in a joking way. Monty and Emerson have
grown close ever since Childermass. They talk to
each other on the phone once a week.

Emerson laughs and then clears his throat a little too
long, causing uncle Monty to grow irritated and bite

t the skin around his nails.

"We destroyed his whistle."

What?

"What?" Monty echoes my thoughts.

"You have to destroy a special personal item so the
spirit can be released. Nine times out of ten, the
demon will just move on. It wouldn't want to waste
its own energy on trying to hurt people. It will just
find another spirit to take over. I mean, you could
destroy the demon too, but you need the demon's
name for that and you know how hard that is. I'd say
to take care of the clown and get the hell out of
dodge."

A few hours after our talk with Emerson, we're
waiting outside of the diner for Rachel and Danni to
show up. All four of us are going to head over to the
only living survivor's house for a chat. Florence
Hartley was eleven-years-old when Grimshaw
kidnapped her from the carnival one Friday night. He
kept her in a shed for days until he was killed. She
was the only kid left alive after everything went
down.

I can't possibly imagine what that would do to someone. When Monty asked our waitress at breakfast about Florence, she said Florence wasn't the same after what happened to her and is known in town as Florence the Loon. I don't think people understand that when you go through something pretty traumatic, that it damages you in a way. After Childermass, I had nightmares for weeks about what happened there and every time we got a call for a case, a part of me wanted to run away from it all.

Rachel's van pulls into the parking lot of the diner and she honks. It's raining like crazy right now Monty pops out his umbrella and we both run underneath it toward her car.

You're not supposed to be here... a voice stops me in my tracks. Knowing it's coming from behind me, I slowly turn to see the little boy from the museum standing outside of the diner. He's standing about ten feet away from me and he looks like he's freezing.

"What do you want from me?" I ask.

ou don't listen. No one ever listens." He shakes his
ead and then vanishes right before my eyes.

Simon, who are you talking to?" I turn and see
onty standing at Rachel's passenger side with the
oor already open. "You're getting soaking wet. Let's
o."

I turn back around to see if the boy is back,
en though I know he's not there. What did he mean
I don't listen? I've never even gotten the chance to
lk to him.

Simon!" Uncle Monty's voice is stern now, so I hurry
er to the van and jump into the back seat next to
anni.

Who were you talking to?" Danni asks. She looks
nfused.

What? You didn't see him?"

Who?" she's making me feel like I'm going crazy.

The little boy," I tell her. She still looks puzzled.

Simon, I didn't see anyone there..." now a worried
ok appears on her face. "You looked like you were
lking to no one."

But he was there... I swear it." Now I'm getting a
ttle confused. How did she *not* see him? She saw the

girl in the tunnel yesterday. We both saw her. This isn't making any sense and I'd be lying if I said I wasn't getting a little scared too.

"I believe you, Simon."

Instead of replying to her, I just stare down at a button on my coat and stay that way the entire ride to Florence's house.

CHAPTER 8:
THE ONLY SURVIVOR

Danni and I are standing on the curb while Monty and Rachel are talking about how they're going to handle this interview. It's pretty cold today but luckily the rain hasn't started yet. The street we're on is eerily quiet except for a dog bark every once in a while and it reminds me a bit of a ghost town.

"Where's Loomis?" I ask Danni to get my mind off of the eeriness. She seems extremely nervous, I'm guessing interviewing victims isn't that common for her.

"He's back at the carnival lot setting up equipment for when we go back into The Clown House. He's a big help. Before he found us, Rachel and I were running our agency on our own and it was getting too much for us. But since he's been doing this for years and has even been on a TV series, it's nice to have him around."

A TV series? No wonder I thought I recognized him.

"Which TV show was he on?" I ask.

"Paranormal Degrees, I think," Danni says.

"Never heard of that one, but I've seen Loomis before, so it was probably that show and I just don't remember." I say.

"They had to cut the TV show because of a train wreck in New York years back. They were doing an investigation on the train and things got out of hand and the train crashed."

I turn to her and my heart drops into my stomach. My parents died in a track wreck in New York and it just so happened to be a demon that caused the crash.

"When did the wreck happen?" I ask.

"Alright guys, let's do this!" Rachel interrupts Danni before she can say anything. "We need to do this before it gets dark. We have to get back to the carnival lot before Loomis loses his mind."

Florence's front door is candy apple red. Funny enough I can actually smell cinnamon and pples coming from the inside of her house. After Monty rings the doorbell a few times, the front door breaks open and reveals a small old woman with red-gray hair in a tight bun with a few straggly pieces hanging over her wrinkled forehead.

"Come in," she says, her voice soft and warm.

The four of us enter her house and almost instantly I'm overcome with supernatural energy. I stop for a second and lean against a wall. I look over and notice Danni is rubbing at her temples. She must be feeling it too. For some strange reason, there is a lot of supernatural energy flowing through Florence's house, almost as if it's full of spirits.

"You two okay?" Rachel asks, concerned. She walks over to Danni and rubs her on the back. "We're only going to be here for a few minutes."

"We'll be okay," Danni says and combs her hair behind her ears, smiling at Rachel. She's right, we'll be okay. It's just a lot of energy for us to take in. The last time I felt something similar to this was in Childermass at the library.

"Come, sit down," Florence says and we obey, taking up the large red couch across from an expensive looking loveseat. Florence takes the loveseat and offers us tea, which we all decline. "It's nice to have visitors."

"As I told you on the phone, we've come to talk to you about your disappearance in 1955." Rachel takes the reins and leads the conversation. For the first time ever Monty doesn't seem to mind. "We've read about it, but we'd like to hear from you if that is okay."

Monty leans forward to say something to Florence.

"You don't seem–"

"Crazy?" Florence smiles and I don't have to look at anyone else to know we've all gone hot red in the face.

"I was going to say dislocated from reality." Nice save, uncle Monty. I would like to reach across the couch and swat him on the back of the head. He's a pro at saying the wrong things at the wrong times.

"You see, when something dark happens to you, people don't know how to handle it, so they ignore you. Pretty soon you develop a reputation as a kook because you don't go out and you claim to see the dead. But I am not a kook. I'm just an old woman who

as almost murdered by a wicked man in a clown suit
hen I was twelve."

'm sorry," I tell her. She turns to me and smiles.

know, Simon." A chill runs down my spine. I'm
inking she knows my name from my Monty and
achel's inquiry, but I can't be sure.

So let's get to it, shall we?" Florence clears her
roat and takes a sip of tea. "It was Halloween night.
was trick-or-treating with several friends of mine
nd while we were going back to the carnival for the
alloween prize raffle, we saw Grimshaw standing on
e side of the road holding a bunch of balloons. He
lled us over and of course, we went. Everyone knew
rimshaw. But something about that night made him
em different somehow. We followed him into the
oods behind the carnival because he said he had
rprises for us because they already announced the
inner of the raffle." Florence takes a tissue out of a
old box and dries her eyes.

We were walking for a long time before we stopped
t the old doll factory, which we called The Clown
ouse. We could hear the carnival still going and
ould hear them announcing a winner to the raffle...
onfused I turned to say something to Grimshaw.

The last thing I remember is seeing his face before woke up chained to a pole in a dark room, which turned out to be a shed. I could hear my friends screaming outside and could smell fire. I cried myse to sleep."

Florence wipes her eyes again and stifles a cry "If it's too much, you can stop," Rachel tells her. Instead of answering, Florence clears her throat and sits up straight.

"I was in that shed for days. I could hear Grimshaw laughing and could feel him in the shed with me. He would tell me I was going to die soon. But I never spoke to him. The night the little boy, Darren Whitehall, told on Grimshaw was the night I was going to be killed. Luckily I was saved from that night. But my friends weren't. I don't leave the hous because I know he's out there. As long as I'm inside, he can't hurt me."

The silence in the living room is pierced by th sudden sound of heavy rain.

"Monty, can I talk to you for a minute?" Rachel taps Monty on the leg and they both get up and follow ach other, through the dining room and into the kitchen, leaving Danni and I with Florence.

"I'm sorry we made you cry," Danni tells Florence.

"Don't worry about that, my dear. I'm a strong woman."

"I believe you," Danni smiles.

"I do, too," I say. Florence looks at me and studies my face.

"Can I use your bathroom?" Danni asks. No wonder she's been tapping her left foot on the floor since we sat down.

"Of course, it's the last door down the hall."

We both watch as Danni hurries down a dim hallway. The bathroom door clicks shut and I turn back to Florence.

"Your parents love you a lot, *little Oso.*"

Shock stuns me and I nearly choke on the air.

"How did you..."

"Your parents spoke to me the day you arrived in town. They asked me to tell you to be strong, even if you don't always feel like it." I smile because I know that she's telling the truth. And Truth be told, I needed to hear that. I just don't know why they couldn't tell me themselves.

"You can speak to the dead, too?" I ask.

"Ever since nearly coming close to death in that she[...] I've been able to speak to the dead, yes. Sometimes [...] let them pass through my house." Now, I know why there's so much energy here. It may be residual, but it's still pretty strong.

"I've been able to since I was eight."

"That's very young to receive the gift."

"I was scared at first," I confess. I've never told anyone this.

"So was I," Florence smiles at me.

"Danni and I saw Natasha Ward in the tunnels of th[...] Clown House yesterday. She seems like a good one." [...] explain.

"Oh, she is a wonderful girl. She was taken so young."

"But I keep seeing this little boy... he told me that Grimshaw was going to get me and then told me to leave town. But the interesting thing is, Danni couldn't see him." I still can't believe she couldn't se[...] the boy.

"That sounds like Darren Whitehall. I see him from time to time. No need to worry, he's a good boy. He's[...]

got a little temper though. He died a few weeks after they caught Grimshaw. I think it was the Flu."

"But why am I the only one who can see him?" I ask, hoping she can help me. If not, I'll have to give Emerson another call when we get back to the motel.

"It sounds to me like he feels attached you. So he's only letting you see him. Spirits can do that sometimes." Florence explains as she drops a few sugar cubes into her tea and stirs it.

"I'm glad I'm not going crazy," I tell her. I am relieved, I almost thought it was some demonic stuff at work again.

"I understand completely." Florence smile at me.

"We're going to get rid of Grimshaw," I tell her.

"I have a feeling you will," she winks at me. "Just please be careful, I don't want to see you or Danni become spirits stuck in this town. There's too many and they all need to be free."

I reach my hand over and take hers.

"I promise, Mrs. Hartley."

A cat meows from somewhere inside the house.

"Oh no, Simon, dear, would you do me a favor and let

Precious in, she's at the back door. Poor love must be soaked."

"Sure," I tell Florence and head to the back door. Unfortunately, Florence is right. Sitting outside of the glass back door is a white cat that is soaked to the bone. I grab the knob and pull the door open. The cat hurries inside and shakes itself underneath the dining room table.

"*Hello...*" I look up and see a little girl in a brown dress standing outside in Florence's backyard. The rain has stopped but she looks drenched from head to toe. She must be one of the many spirits Florence lets through her house.

I go outside and head down the concrete steps to the back lawn. The girl is across the yard now, standing at a laundry clothing line with sheets hanging from it. I lift my camera up and take a quick picture of the clothing line. A gust of wind picks up and the sheets dance in the cold breeze.

"Are you passing through?" I ask her.
"He hurts us real bad when we talk to live people... I have to go now." The little girl turns and runs

rough the sheets.

"Wait!" I call out. "Come back! Who hurts you?" I
push my way through the sheets and end up on the
other side. She's gone.

A rattle of laughter shakes me in place and I know
exactly who it is. *Be strong*, I tell myself and turn
around. The sheets are blowing in the wind but I can
see Grimshaw's silhouette behind each sheet.

Before I can tell myself to stop, I do something
stupid. I run into the sheets and yank each of them
down trying to find the stupid clown. Just as I'm
about to rip the last one down, the wind picks up and
Grimshaw's laughter is so close, I can feel his breath
the back of my neck.

I turn to face him, but I'm stopped by the sheet as it
wraps itself around my neck, growing tighter and
tighter. It yanks me upward and my feet are dangling
above the ground. It doesn't take me long to realize
I'm practically being strangled by a ghost.

This is totally not how I'd like to die.

Grimshaw's laughter grows louder and louder and the sheet grows tighter. I can feel my face going purple and can hear ringing in my ears along with Grimshaw's chilling laughter.

"Go away!" I hear a voice scream near me and I recognize it as Danni's. "Go away!" she screams even louder and almost instantly I'm released and dropped to the soaking wet grass.

I try to catch my breath as Monty and Rachel hurry over to me and Monty lifts me up from the ground.

"What the hell happened, Simon?"

"It was Grimshaw," Danni says.

"This is getting out of hand," Rachel tells Monty. "We were just talking in the kitchen about this. Once the kids get hurt, we quit."

"We can't quit," I say, my throat is a little sore. "We have to do get rid of Grimshaw. This town will never be safe until he's gone."

"Simon's right," Danni agrees.

Monty and Rachel share concerned looks.

"Then we do it tonight," Rachel says. "The faster we get rid of Grimshaw, the faster we'll get the heck out of this town."

"Are you sure about this, Simon?" Monty asks me.

Rubbing my sore neck I turn to the back door and see Florence standing on the other side of the glass. She looks worried and sad.

"I'm sure and I know exactly what we need to do."

CHAPTER 9:
ONE LAST STOP

The four of us are back at the Pottinger Public Library, but just our freaking luck it's closed today. The rain is coming down harder than ever and the adrenaline in me is not going to let the fact that the library is closed stop me from doing what I need to do.

"What exactly are we doing here again?" Monty asks, turning to me in the backseat.

"The hat, it's a personal item, Monty. Emerson said we have to destroy a personal item of the spirit and what better than Grimshaw's signature top hat?"

'But how are we going to get it if the library is closed?" Rachel asks as she stares at the library through the wet windshield.

"We're going to have to break the law... a little."

"*A little*?" Monty's voice screeches like a tire.

"Simon, that's breaking and entering."

"And theft, if we take the hat," Rachel adds.

"But we need it, this is a matter of life and death. I think the Mayor would understand. He's paying us to get rid of Grimshaw and that's exactly what we're trying to do." I'm trying my best to explain it so that they understand the severity of the situation. If we don't get the hat, there's no point in going back to The Clown House. We'd basically be walking into a trap and I'm not going through that again.

"He's right," Danni finally pipes up. "We need to get rid of Grimshaw before he kills more people. This can work."

"Dang it," Rachel exhales and looks at the library once again. "How are we going to get in? We don't have any tools to break into a building."

"Simon," Danni nudges me in the shoulder and points out of the window. "Look, it's Natasha."

I switch my gaze from Rachel and follow Danni's finger. Across the parking lot, standing right in front of the library's entrance is Natasha, the spirit who has been the most help so far.

"I have an idea," I tell Monty and Rachel. "Danni and

will get the hat and you two head back to the
carnival lot and help Loomis set up a something so
can destroy the hat."

Monty looks at me like I'm insane.
"Leave you here?" Monty shakes his head. "No."
"We'll be fine. The carnival lot is two blocks away,
we'll be there in no time. Trust me, Monty." I know
he trusts me, but I might be stretching that trust a
little far with what I'm asking of him. I haven't been
without him by my side since Childermass. I'm not
even sure I know what I'm doing.
"Fine," Monty says.
"But get your butts back to the lot when you're
done." Rachel jumps in and glares at Danni and I,
seemingly trying to intimidate us. Monty takes a note
out of her book and copies Rachel's glare, though
Monty looks like he needs to use the restroom more
than anything.

"We promise," Danni and I say in unison.
As the van drives away, Danni and I jog across
the parking lot to the front of the library and squeeze
underneath an eave where it's dry and warm. The

spirit of Natasha Ward is leaning against the wall and she has her arms crossed like she's annoyed wit something.

"No one ever listens to me or Darren. We try our be to get people like you to get the heck out of town, b you always end up dead. It's so annoying."

"We're going to destroy him, Natasha," I tell her. "We just need his hat to do it."

She turns to us with a confused look on her face.

"Why do you need his hat?"

"Because if we destroy it, it will get rid of him," Danni adds, squeezing the rainwater out of her ponytail. "We just need to get it from inside the museum."

"I think I can help with that," Natasha smirks and without saying another word walks through the from doors and unlocks them for us.

The inside of the library is surprisingly warm as if they have the heat on and I appreciate it. Outside, the rain felt like ice and my teeth hurt from them chattering so much.

Silently we follow Natasha down a hallway to

the museum. Before Natasha can open the door, someone else does.

"I've been looking for you," the little boy says.

"Darren, I've been trying to find you for days."

Natasha hurries over to Darren and takes him into her arms. It's a sad and happy moment because they're dead, but they've grown so close in the afterlife that it almost seems like they're siblings.

"I thought I told you to leave," Darren says over Natasha's shoulder.

"This is the boy you were talking about?" Danni asks. Finally, she can see him, which means he must be comfortable with her now.

"Yeah, he's been trying to help but-"

"You don't listen. He is going to hurt all of you... but right now he's going to start with your other friends."

"Wait, what did you say?" Danni says to Darren. He shakes his head again and then lets go of Natasha.

"He has your friends right now in the tunnels... he's waiting for you."

"Oh my god, Monty, Rachel, and Loomis!" Danni starts to cry. "Simon, we have to get the hat and hurry."

I feel like this is all my fault. It was my idea for
them to go ahead of us and now that freaking clown
has them trapped down there.

"This is all my freaking fault," I kick the wall.

"No, it's not, Simon." Danni looks at me. "It's
Grimshaw's."

"You'll both be walking into a trap," Natasha
explains. "But we can help to an extent. Just tell us
what you need to do."

"We need to burn that hat," I tell her.

"There's a gas station across the street, you can get
some stuff from there to build a fire," Natasha
explains.

A phone rings and sends Danni and I on a fit of
screams. The ringtone is Monty's and I remember I
have his phone.

I yank the phone out of my jacket pocket and see that
it is Emerson calling. Quickly, before it goes to
voicemail, I answer it and put it on speaker mode.

"Emerson," I breathe out. "Just the person we need."

"Simon," Emerson says and his voice sounds different

ike he's about to say something I don't want to hear. You and Monty need to get out of that town *right now*."

"Emerson, Monty is sort of trapped in a mine tunnel with a demented clown ghost right now." Emerson curses so loud over the phone that Danni flinches across the hallway.

"Simon, listen to me. Monty told me about the other investigators that were there helping you get rid of the clown. I knew when he told me their names that one stuck out like a sore thumb... Loomis. Loomis Strode. He was a part of the same team your parents were on back in the day. When they helped him investigate that Burlington Train haunting in New York... he was helping Madolock. He helped kill your parents, Simon."

I have to lean against the wall to steady myself because I know I will faint if I don't. My head is throbbing now and my chest is hurting. After I told myself over and over that I would never let this happen to me again, it has and I can't help but feel a little defeated.

"What? no..." Danni says, shaking her head. "He's

our friend... *he can't be...*"

"Simon, I'm sorry, but you have to get out of town. He may be human, but he works with demons, he's not the type to go messing with." Emerson explains. "He'll kill you if he gets the chance."

"I can't leave Monty and Rachel down there, Emerson. We're going to destroy Grimshaw's hat like you said, a personal item. We're literally ten feet away from it.

"The Clown House," Emerson says. "It's where he died the first time, it's the perfect place. The burning of his hat will draw his spirit out to the hat and he'll be bound to it forever. You have to be quick about it, tomorrow is Halloween and you won't stand a chance against Grimshaw."

I think about my parents and all the betrayal I've gone through. I can't keep letting these things win. I can't keep letting myself get dragged down by evil spirits and two-faced people. Loomis has no idea what's coming for him, neither does Grimshaw.

"I can do this, Emerson. I know I can."

"Godspeed, my boy. Be careful."

"I promise," I tell Emerson and hang up.

What do we do now?" Danni says.

Alright, let's grab the hat and head to the house before it gets dark. We're going to burn this freaking down to the ground."

CHAPTER 10:
RETURN TO THE CLOWN HOUSE

The rain has let up as we hastily move throug the woods toward The Clown House. Danni still can believe Loomis is bad and I don't blame her, I couldn't believe it when the same thing happened to me in Childermass.

While we're headed to the tunnels to save Monty and Rachel, lighter fluid and matches from the gas station in tow, Natasha and Darren have the hat and should already be at the house ready to star the fire.

The Clown House comes into view and chills spin down my spine. Looking up at the house feels different now, it feels like I'm right back at the Childermass library.

My chest begins to hurt and my throat feels like its closing up. But I have to be strong, I'm a Santiago, and Santiagos don't give up. We fight.

"I'm sorry about what Loomis did to your parents," Danni tells me. I turn to her and put my hand on her shoulder.

"I've only known you for a few days but I feel like we're best friends already. Loomis isn't your fault, he's evil."

Danni smiles at me and I know she feels a little better now. A loud creaking snatches our attention and we turn to the front door of the house. Natasha and Darren walk out of the front door with Grimshaw's hat and nod at us.

"It's ready."

Walking into The Clown House again doesn't feel right, there's so much more energy here than the last time and it's making me a bit lightheaded. Danni looks like she feels the same since she keeps stopping and sitting on the railings of the old beds.

Sitting in the middle of the room is a makeshift pit made out rocks and sticks. For two ghosts, Natasha and Darren did a pretty good job at gathering human world items, usually it takes a lot of power for spirit to do that.

"Alright, this is how we're going to do this," I say. "Danni and I are going to go down into the tunnels get Monty and Rachel. After we get them, Danni is going to call Monty's phone and when you hear it ring, light Grimshaw's hat on fire in this pit."

I put Monty's phone on the ground and make sure it's got enough battery for this plan.

"Okay," Natasha says. "We can do that."

"Your mom and dad said to be careful, little Oso," Darren says to me.

I turn back to him and smile.

"Tell them I said, I *promise*."

Getting back down into the tunnels is the easy part, but navigating our way down here with just Danni's phone's flashlight is harder than we thought. The mining cart tracks below keep making me trip. The last thing I need is a twisted ankle while trying to get away from an evil clown ghost,

I can't see anything," I tell Danni.

Wait," Danni says. "I think I see something." She points her phone's flashlight toward a square panel on the wall a few feet in front of us.

We hurry up to the panel, my shoe catching on the tracks every now and again. She flashes the light on the panel. A piece of duct tape on the front reads: *Lighting/Elect.* and I want to hug Danni.

"Hopefully it still works," I say, hoping it still has some juice.

Danni opens the panel and a dozen white switches covered in dust appear.

"A lot of Mines used to run on generators, so if we're lucky," she says as she grabs one of the switches and yanks it upward. "We'll get some light." Almost instantly the tunnels are lit with single bulbs dangling from the ceiling. It's not perfect lighting but it's a whole lot better than the phone.

"Alright, let's get Monty and Rachel and get the heck out of here," I say.

"Not so fast, you two." A familiar voice echoes from behind us.

Danni and I turn and see a clown standing a

89

good hundred feet from us. But this clown isn't Grimshaw. It has the clown mask on, the one I took a picture of the first time we came down here. This clown is also bulky and scarier looking than Grimshaw.

"*Loomis?*" Danni says.

The clown tilts its head to the side and then swings a pickaxe into the air, popping a few light bulbs. The clown takes a few steps forward and pops another round of bulbs. The clown laughs and then lunges forward toward us.

"RUN!" I grab Danni and pull her down the tunnel. We both charge further down the tunnels and just like I predicted, my shoe catches on a track and I fall chest first toward the ground.

"Simon, get up!" Danni is trying to pull me up, but I already know there's something wrong with my ankle. "I think I hear them calling out to us."

I listen closely and can hear Monty calling my name. He's alright. That's all I need to know.

"Give me your phone," I tell her. Without asking why she hands it to me.

We haven't got Rachel and Monty yet, Simon."

"I'll hold him off and you go find them. Yell out to me when you've got them and I will call Monty's phone."

"Simon, no! Loomis is going to kill you." She starts to cry.

"No, he won't. Now, go!" I tell her. "GO!"

Danni gives me one last look with tears streaming down her face and then she takes off down the tunnels, leaving me alone with a deranged clown with a giant pickaxe.

Funny enough, I'm not that scared anymore. I've been through so much in my life that I'm tired of being scared. I push myself up against a wall and lift myself off the ground, trying not to step down on my left ankle.

The clown stops a few feet away from me and he chuckles.

"You're pathetic, you know that?" I tell the clown. "These demons you help don't care about you."

"You don't know anything, boy!" the clown speaks

from behind the mask.

"They only like power and you're just giving it to them at no cost. What do you get out of it? *Loomis*. You'll always be human, you can't have power, it doesn't work like that, you idiot!"

"SHUT UP!" the clown screams and yanks his mask off. "I've been bringing kids here to sacrifice them t Grimshaw for years and I have power because of it. You're just like your parents, Simon Santiago. They didn't get it and neither do you."

"Nope, *you* don't get it, Loomis. Killing people for demons don't give you power. They've been tricking you. Grimshaw isn't a demon. He's just a regular spirit who has been being used by one. So, what demon are *you* talking about?" I know asking for the demon's name is the stupidest idea ever, but I'm all out of ideas for today.

"Klarvis needs me!" he yells back at me. His face is hot red now. No way, it actually worked.

"*Klarvis*?" I ask and the smile on his face falls. He's realizing what he's done and I hope Danni finds the in time before he really tries to kill me.

"You listen to me, boy!" Loomis snaps at me. "I'm going to kill you..."

Remembering the rules I made for myself for ...ses after Childermass, I frantically search my ...cket's inside pockets and want to cry out in ...ppiness when my hand latches around a mini bottle ...holy water and the rosary my mom gave to me ...hen I was little.

I yank both of them out and Loomis takes ...veral steps back, realizing what I have in my hand. ...can hear footsteps behind me.

...imon, I found them." I turn and see Danni standing ...ith Monty and Rachel. Monty smiles at me and ...ods, giving his silent approval for whatever I'm ...bout to do.

I drench the rosary in the holy water and smile ...t Loomis.

...Please, don't. I can get you more power, Simon. ...ou'll be stronger than your parents ever were." ...oomis doesn't look so scary anymore; he looks like a ...urt child.

...I've got all the power I need," I tell him and slam the

rosary against the rock wall. "KLARVIS... IN THE NAME OF THE FATHER, THE SON, AND THE HOLY SPIRIT... I BANISH YOU FROM HERE!"

Almost instantly, the light bulbs begin to explode one by one and the walls begin to rumble. We need to get out of here, *now*.

"Let's go!" I yell out and limp toward the steps. Monty grabs hold of me and helps me.

"I'm proud of you, Simon. I hate to admit this but you've got more cajones than me when it comes to stuff like this." Monty laughs.

Instead of responding, I just laugh with him. I really don't know what I'd do without him; it scares me to even think about it sometimes.

As we near the steps leading out of the tunnel a clown is blocking our way. But this time, it's Grimshaw. His chuckles turn into growls as he head toward us. He's trying to trap us down here.

"Hey Grimshaw," I say and the clown stops in his tracks. I take out Danni's phone and a giant grin spreads across my face. "You like tricks, don't you? Well, I've got one specifically just for you." I hit the all button on Danni's phone.

From where we are I can hear Monty's phone ringing. Grimshaw, angrier with me stalks forward and I can see now that he's dragging an actual ax behind him.

"What are we going to do?" Rachel cries from behind me.

"Just wait," I smile. Not knowing Natasha and Darren all that well, I'd trust them with my life and I know my parents would too.

Grimshaw lifts the ax into the air and before he can swing it down on us, the sadistic smile leaves his face and the ax falls to the ground with a clatter. Not really understanding what's going on, the clown stumbles backward and starts to laugh. He begins to flicker like a dying candle flame and then vanishes from our sight.

With the tunnels still falling apart, we all rush up the steps and back into the house. I linger behind with Monty.

"We've got to get out of here, Simon," Monty says.

I turn around, knowing that there's still one more clown down in the tunnels. A few feet away Loomis is standing there. He looks disappointed and heartbroken and even though I will hate myself forever, I feel a little bad for him. But then something changes, his look of sadness turns into a look of rage. He turns around and begins walking back down the tunnels.

"Simon, we have to go!" Monty pulls me up the steps and into the house. Before he can close the door to the tunnels, a load of rocks fills up the hole in the floor like a wall. Even though a part of me still feels bad for Loomis, we finally did what we came here to do.

We helped this town when it needed us the most and that makes everything a hundred times better. It makes me feel a hundred times better.

EPILOGUE: ONE YEAR LATER

One thing has changed since that night in Pottinger, Monty isn't afraid of clowns anymore. But then again, it's only been a year since we got rid of Grimshaw.

The town is doing better now, Natasha and Darren moved on and they even got rid of that stupid Grimshaw section in the museum.

Danni and Rachel have become a part of our agency, I mean since Monty and Rachel are married now it wouldn't make sense having two competing agencies in one house. Oh yeah, we finally have a house... well, a mobile one but it's still *home* to me.

I thought that after Childermass, I would never feel good again. I thought I'd always feel sad and afraid to keep going. But my parents once told

e that I'm needed in this world to help people with
heir paranormal troubles and I know now why I have
his gift and why I need to keep using it.

Things happen in life that we can't see coming
and instead of cowering and hiding from all the
problems that life brings us, we need to face them
head on and get through. It makes us stronger and
when we're stronger, we can get through anything...
even gross ghost ectoplasm.

THE END...

THANK YOU!

I had a lot of fun writing this duology for you. I felt so close to Simon as a character and building his relationship with Monty was one of my favorite parts of writing these books, aside from the awesome ghostly fun. I want to thank all of you for loving The Ghost Talker Files. The story is over for now. But you never know, there could be more stories to tell in the future.

\- Richard Denney

TURN THE PAGE
FOR SOME
AWESOME EXTRA
PHOTOS FROM
SIMON'S CAMERA!